Nana's Quilt

Stitched in St. John's, Newfoundland and Labrador

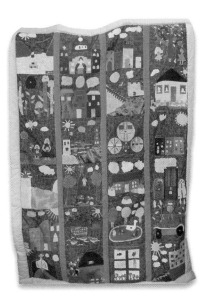

Written by Lori Lane and Kathy Winsor

Photography by Jim Costello

Tuckamore Bo
a Creative Publishers impr

St. John's, Newfoundland and L   ador
2005

We acknowledge the support of The Canada Council for the Arts for our publishing program.

We acknowledge the financial support of the Government of Canada through the Book Publishing Industry Development Program (BPIDP) for our publishing program.

Cover Photo by Jim Costello
Cover Design and Layout by Todd Manning
Printed on acid-free paper

Published by
TUCKAMORE BOOKS
an imprint of CREATIVE BOOK PUBLISHING
a Transcontinental associated company
P.O. Box 8660, St. John's, Newfoundland and Labrador A1B 3T7

Printed in Canada by:
Transcontinental Inc.
2nd Printing, October 2005

Library and Archives Canada Cataloguing in Publication

Lane, Lori, 1962-
    Nana's Quilt: Stitched in St. John's, Newfoundland and Labrador/ written by Lori Lane and Kathy Winsor; photography by Jim Costello.

ISBN 1-894294-82-3

    1. St. John's (N.L.)—History—Juvenile fiction. 2. St. John's (N.L.)—Description and travel—Juvenile fiction. I. Winsor, Kathy, 1960- II. Costello, Jim III. Title.

PS8623.A522N35 2005   jC813'.6   C2005-900816-4

This book became a reality through the funding of our ArtsSmarts Project 2003/2004. Our community of children and teachers at Hazelwood Elementary, supported by local artists and parents, created visual representations of our historic city, St. John's, Newfoundland and Labrador.

The ongoing support and interest from numerous people added to the enthusiasm of this creative adventure.

Many thanks to our local artists: Penny Wooding for plasticine modeling of Lester's Farm with Kindergartens; Jackie Ryan for quilting around the city with grade ones; Undrea Norris for paper collage of Bowring Park with grade twos; Pat Ryan for watercolour painting of Quidi Vidi with grade threes, as well as her support and insistence that this project could be done. Thank you, Pat, we did it; Elizabeth Tucker for rug hooking with grade fours; Elayne Greeley for acrylic painting on wooden row houses with grade fives and Sheilagh O'Leary for black and white photography of churches with grade sixes.

A special thank you to our school's secretaries, Mrs. Trixie Wight and Mrs. Sharen Furlong. They have taken a personal interest in this project.

Thank you to Ken Murphy from the Newfoundland and Labrador Arts Council for his support and encouragement.

Thank you to our school principal, Veronica Mahoney, for recognizing the importance and value of ArtsSmarts and providing the necessary support to carry out the program.

We also need to recognize the patience of Sister Madeline Kehoe and Kya Dooley. During the many photo shoots, they were always ready for "just one more."

Kathy and Lori would like to extend a great big thank you to the following people for their support, patience and guidance during the many hours of writing and rewriting: Jim Costello, Ed Kavanagh, Nora Flynn, Donna Francis, Angela Pitcher, Todd Manning, Hazelwood Staff, Kathy's son Benjamin and Lori's family, Aprille, William and Patrick Balsom.

School was out for the summer! Everyone was excited about vacation. Everyone except me!

"No way, Mom!" I yelled. "I'm not going back to daycare like some . . . baby." I could barely see through my tears. "And there are no kids over by Nana's. It's not fair!"

"Allie—"

"You said we were going to see Auntie in England."

Mom sighed. "I'm sorry. But Dad and I have to work. And you're not old enough to be left on your own. Nana said you could come to her house during the day. It's either that or daycare. You decide."

I turned on my heels and ran to my room.

I love my Nana very much, but I was so looking forward to getting off this island and going somewhere interesting for a holiday. My best friend, Rebecca, was going to Florida with her family, and Anna Marie, up the street, was driving to Toronto with her Dad. I could imagine getting back to school in September and the teacher asking about our summer vacation. What would I say? I stayed home!

I didn't know it at the time, but I was about to have a summer I would never forget. Nana, you see, had plans up her sleeve.

Monday, June 28th

It was early when I got to Nana's house. I quietly opened the front door not knowing if Nana and Poppy would be up, but the wind slammed the screen door shut behind me. Oops!

"I'm in here, Allie," Nana called.

I dropped my backpack with a clunk on the porch floor. I had my CD player, CDs, magazines, movies and lots of other stuff. Everything I would need to get through the day. I walked down the hall to the backroom where Nana was going through her bags of fabric. It looked like she'd been sorting and cutting for days.

"What's all this for?" I asked. "Are you making another quilt?"

Nana looked up at me. "Yes," she said. "But I thought maybe you and I could work on this one. We have all summer."

Was she kidding?

"Oh, that's okay, Nana. I'm not really into sewing." But she didn't seem to hear. She continued to arrange her fabric in colourful bundles, patting each one down firmly.

"We need to get started right away," she insisted, brushing the threads from her sweater. "Now go out to the kitchen. Poppy has bologna and eggs in the pan. You need a good hearty breakfast this morning."

I looked at her curiously. "Why?"

"Because you and I are going for a nice long walk up Signal Hill. That's where we'll find the first block for our quilt."

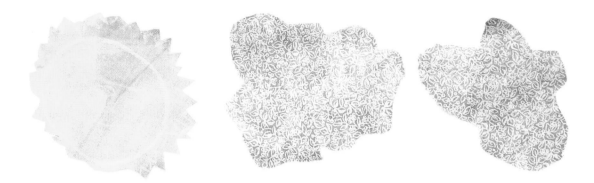

What could Signal Hill have to do with a quilt? But I knew there was no point arguing. When Nana makes up her mind about something, it stays made up. While I sat eating, and Poppy finished his cup of tea, Nana scurried around putting things in her backpack. It looked like we'd be gone for quite a while.

Poppy put his cup in the sink. "Where are my two favourite girls going today?"

I shrugged and pointed out the window. "Up there."

The tower at the top of Signal Hill always looked so far away from Nana's kitchen window. I couldn't imagine walking up that long steep hill. My parents always took our car when we visited Cabot Tower. But Nana seemed determined to explore it on foot.

Poppy drove us as far as the Johnson Geo Center parking lot. "I'll meet you back here at one o'clock."

One o'clock! Maybe I should have gone to daycare.

"Take a look around," Nana said, as Poppy drove away. "People come from all corners of the earth for this. Blue sky, clean air, majestic hills—isn't it beautiful?"

"Whatever," I muttered. I was thinking about a field trip our class had taken here last year. Now that was interesting! The walls of the Johnson Geo Center are made of rocks older than dinosaurs.

Nana picked up her backpack and motioned for me to follow. "We'll take this path," she said, pointing to a marked trail near the Interpretation Centre. We trudged along to where we could look out over the ocean cliffs. "Stay close," Nana warned.

We looked down on St. John's Harbour. Nana pointed out fishing boats, tour boats, sailboats and even a cruise ship. "Nana, how could that large ship get through that little opening?" I asked, looking back over my shoulder.

She explained that the entrance to St. John's Harbour is indeed very tight. "I guess that's why they call it 'The Narrows,'" she said. "Sometimes the larger boats have to be guided through by smaller pilot boats."

The Fort Amherst lighthouse on the other side looked very close. "I guess that lighthouse helps when it's foggy."

"Oh, yes," Nana agreed. "Lighthouses have guided many captains safely home—including your grandfather." Nana sighed. "Today many lighthouses are either automated or closed up. I know it's supposed to be progress, but it's such a shame."

Nana headed briskly up the hill. I was having a hard time keeping up. "Nana, wait for me," I called. "How come you walk so fast?"

She laughed. "I come here all the time with your Auntie Pauline. We know these trails well." She took my hand. "Come on. You're as slow as cold molasses."

We climbed some wooden stairs. At the top, we looked out over the ocean. There, rising out of the icy blue water, was a tall, pointed iceberg. I had seen icebergs before, but never this close.

"It's so big, and it sparkles!"

"Yes, and we're only seeing a small part of it. Most of it is under the water."

"How did it get here?" I asked.

"Icebergs float down from the Arctic. It takes about three years for them to make their way to Newfoundland." Nana laughed. "They're almost as slow as you!"

I heard the excitement from a couple of tourists who were pointing and taking pictures. Nana and I walked over and said hello. They had come all the way from Australia hoping to see icebergs and whales.

"Where are the whales?" one tourist asked.

"It's probably too early for whales," Nana said. "You'll have to wait until later in the summer, after the water warms and the caplin are more plentiful."

Nana winked.

"It's a good excuse to come back for another visit."

We finally made it to the top of the hill. I took a deep breath and looked around. I remembered how far away Cabot Tower looked from Nana's window. "I wonder if we can see your house, Nana?" She didn't hear me. She was already sitting on a bench setting out sandwiches and lemonade.

Nana told me stories about Marconi, who sent the first wireless signals across the Atlantic, and how John Cabot came to our island. "That stone building," Nana said, pointing back toward Cabot Tower, "was built in 1897. It's the city's most famous landmark. We'll take a little tour one of these days."

After lunch we wandered around the hill. The sun was warm but it was windy and I was glad to have my sweater. Where had the time gone? Poppy would soon pick us up.

"Allie, look at the fog rolling in," Nana said. "It won't take long for things to cool down. Let's head back to the parking lot."

Wednesday, July 7th

I was tired when I awoke, but I didn't complain too much about having to get up. Nana said we would be staying home today. I was hoping to watch one of my movies.

When I arrived at Nana's, I could hear Poppy clanging dishes in the kitchen and singing. "What would you like for breakfast?" he called out.

"Doesn't matter." I wasn't really interested in eating.

"Blueberry pancakes okay?" Maybe I was a little hungry. Poppy's blueberry pancakes are world famous. Well, at least in our family.

Nana had her sewing machine set up on the backroom table and stacks of fabric all laid out. "We've got lots to keep us busy today, Allie." She was cutting large blue squares and putting them to the side. "We'll use these for our back- ground."

"Your grandmother tells me you're making a quilt," Poppy said when I sat down to the table. "A big one," he chuckled. "She says you'll be sewing your way around the city."

Thursday, July 15th

Every summer on the first Wednesday of August my family heads to Quidi Vidi Lake for the Royal St. John's Regatta. It wasn't Wednesday or even August, so I was surprised when Nana asked Poppy to drive us to Quidi Vidi Village.

"There's a fine breeze blowing out there today," Poppy said as we drove by Quidi Vidi Lake. I could see a family of ducks huddled close to the shore, bobbing up and down on the water.

"They must be cold, Poppy."

"Oh, don't worry about them. They're used to wild weather," he assured me. Near the end of the lake, Poppy pulled over to the side of the road.

"How about this, girls? From here

you can walk down to the Village in about two minutes."

"Aren't you coming?" I asked, opening the car door.

"Not today, Allie. I've got to get your grandmother's new flower boxes finished." Poppy grinned. "Now keep an eye on her. Don't let her get too close to the water's edge."

"When are you coming back?"

Poppy gave me a reassuring wink. "Oh, soon enough."

"We have lots of time to stroll around today," Nana said. She looked out over the lake and smiled. "Down here you'd never even know you were in a city."

Yes," I said. "The water and hills make it look more like out around the bay where Uncle Will lives."

We made our way into the Village. "The roads are so narrow," I said. "It must be hard for cars to pass each other."

"You're right," said Nana. "It's almost as if things haven't changed here in two hundred years." Nana stopped and pointed. "There's something I want to show you over there," she said, heading straight towards a pretty little house. "It's believed to be one of the oldest cottages in North America."

"It doesn't look very old."

"Ah, but it is," Nana said. "This is Mallard Cottage. It was built in 1750, but the owners have done some repairs and made some changes. They've kept the roof the same, though. Notice how it comes way down over the sides? It's called a 'hipped' roof. You don't see many houses built like that nowadays."

Nana knocked and a friendly looking woman opened the cottage door. "Good morning, ladies," she said, standing back. "Come on in, I'm just opening up."

Wow! I had never seen so much stuff in someone's house before. There were knick-knacks on tables and shelves and in the windows. My eyes tried to take it all in. "Nana, what does she do with all this?" I whispered.

"She sells it," Nana answered. "They're mostly antiques and collectibles."

I picked up a little red and white dish in the shape of a tomato. I couldn't resist lifting the lid to peek inside. "Careful, Allie," Nana said, placing the dish back on the window ledge. "You wouldn't want to break anything. Some of these pieces are one of a kind and very valuable!"

"You mean, like Poppy?" I said, smiling. I could tell she knew what I meant.

After exploring Mallard Cottage we walked around the rest of the Village. It was so cosy! Some houses and gardens looked like they had come out of a

storybook. Nana showed me the tiny old church that someone had turned into a house.

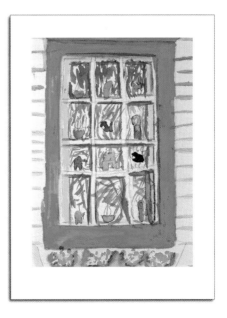

I soon felt a rumbling in my stomach. I didn't see any place to buy fries or a burger, but of course Nana had come prepared. I followed her down to the water where we sat on some flat rocks. It was a nice place to have a picnic.

"Do you know another name for Quidi Vidi Village?" Nana asked.

"No."

"It's called the Gut—or at least the water part of it is."

I laughed. "That's a funny name."

Nana nodded. "Places in Newfoundland often have funny names."

I wondered about the small wooden buildings all along the water's edge. "Are they cabins, Nana?"

"No. They're storehouses—sheds where fishermen keep their fishing gear. You'll still see them all over Newfoundland. What you don't see as often are flakes."

"What are flakes?"

"Wooden platforms. Years ago, people would lay salted fish out on the flakes to dry. That's how they preserved it for the winter. Salt fish makes a fine meal of fish and brewis."

"Fish and brewis!" Sometimes Mom makes that. "Yuck!"

The low murmur of a motor echoed in the cove. "Listen," Nana whispered. The sound was getting closer. We could see a small fishing boat carefully making its way through a narrow opening in the rocks.

"Another fisherman is safely home, Allie." Nana stood up and gave a little wave as the boat puttered along in front of us. "I wouldn't want to be out there on the mighty Atlantic Ocean today," she said.

"Why not?" I asked. "The water is so calm."

"It's calm here in the Gut, but that's because it's protected by all these hills. But just out through those cliffs are huge whitecaps on the ocean. Remember how windy it was for the ducks on Quidi Vidi Lake?"

I held Nana's hand as we walked back to meet Poppy. "Are we going to make pictures of Quidi Vidi for the quilt?" I asked.

"Indeed we are," Nana said, giving my hand a little squeeze.

15

Tuesday, July 27th

Nana was taking me to visit her friend, Mabel. She rushed around the house, searching under pillows, along the mantlepiece, and opening and closing cupboards.

"Nana, what are you looking for?" I asked when she came into the kitchen.

"My new rhubarb pickle recipe. I promised Mabel I'd bring it for her."

"Is this it?" I asked, taking a yellow index card from behind a magnet on the fridge.

Nana grinned. "I knew I'd put it somewhere."

"Allie, you might want to take a book or movie with you," Poppy said, smiling. "When those girls get together no one else can get a word in edgewise. I don't know what they've got left to talk about."

"Never mind your grandfather," Nana said. "He's just afraid Mabel and I talk about him."

Riding the bus to Mabel's house was fun. I hadn't been on the Metrobus since last year. "You know, Allie, "said Nana, "Mabel and I have been best friends since we were your age. When I'm with her, it feels like only yesterday when we were running through the downtown streets and laneways," she laughed. "Do you know what the row of houses where Mabel lives is called?"

"No."

"Jelly Bean Row. See if you can guess why."

As soon as we stepped off the bus I knew what she meant. The houses were beautiful, bright colours—lime-green, raspberry-red—just like the colours of jelly beans. And Mabel's house was one of the nicest—a lovely ocean blue.

Mabel met us at the door, wiping her hands on her apron. "Just what I like to see," Nana said, stepping inside. "A sign that you've been baking." Walking down the hall to the kitchen, we could smell bread. Six freshly baked loaves, just greased with buttered paper, were lined up on the counter.

"Now, let me get you a cup of tea and some milk for Allie," Mabel said, taking her dishes down from the cupboard.

"Sounds lovely," said Nana.

"Slice of hot bread, Allie?" Mabel asked, carefully tearing two buns of bread apart. "I don't know why, but the 'kissing slice' is my favourite—the slice cut from where the buns of a loaf join together." We put butter and homemade blueberry jam on each slice. The smell was heavenly, but the taste . . . mmm!

I sat at the kitchen table a while longer, but Poppy was right. I didn't get much chance to speak. Nana and Mabel talked and laughed so much they were wiping tears from their eyes.

I went outside and waited on the front step. Nana warned me to be careful because there was no porch or yard, and the street was right there in front of me. The houses were all joined together and lined up in neat little rows. Each house was painted a different colour. I played a game in my mind. If I were to choose a house to live in, which would I pick? Maybe I would make mine a different colour. I opened the pencil box that I carried in my backpack and flicked through the coloured crayons. I took out a bright yellow one and drew a tall rectangular box. It was flat on top with little squares or circles for windows. I coloured it carefully, pressing hard to make the colours bright.

Nana startled me when she opened the door. "Oh, now isn't that a lovely picture," she said, looking down at my drawing. "Hold on to that and we'll use it as a pattern for a quilt block."

As we were leaving, Mabel gave us some leftover bread dough and said, "Poppy can fry up some toutons for you." Yum! Now that was more like it! Much better than fish and brewis.

During the bus ride home I was careful not to wrinkle my picture. I thought about all the brightly colored fabric Nana had. There were lots of nice colours to make pictures of Mabel's house.

Summer was passing quickly. Rebecca was back from Florida. We got to see each other on the weekend, but then her family headed to Summerville to see her Nanny Tilley. Oh well.

I never knew what plans my Nana would have for us. Some days we would just stay around her house. We would work on blocks for the quilt or do chores in her garden. Nana always kept us busy, that's for sure!

Friday, August 6th

Today when I arrived at Nana's, she was already dressed to go out. "Allie," she said, taking my hand, "we're going to church."

"Church! Church is for Sundays."

But if that's what Nana had in mind . . .

"Which one?" I asked, trying to keep the disappointment out of my voice.

"Well, we'll start with the Basilica. It won't take long to walk there."

We set out and soon I caught a glimpse of a huge clock tower.

"This is the Basilica of St. John the Baptist," Nana said. "It's one of the oldest and most recognized buildings in St. John's."

Inside the hollow stone porch we were greeted by large wooden doors. Reaching up, I pulled back on one of the handles, and slowly squeezed inside.

I stopped and stood in silent awe.

It was so big! The bright sunlight shone through the stained glass windows. I didn't know where to look.

We stepped inside, our footsteps echoing. Nana and I sat in a wooden pew. It was so quiet, until, as if by magic, organ music filled the entire space.

"What luck!" Nana said. "The organist must be practising today." She showed me the brochure she had taken from a table on her way in. It said that the organ was the largest musical instrument in Newfoundland and has 4050 pipes. That would explain the beautiful music—and how loud it was.

We peeked into all the archways and looked at the many statues. And the ceiling, it was so fancy with all the gold. I wondered if it was real gold.

"We'd better get going," Nana whispered, glancing at her watch.

Outside I was surprised by the view directly in front of us. "Look, we can see Signal Hill from here."

Nana smiled. "Come on," she said. "Let's take a look at the statue of John the Baptist." We wandered down to where he was standing atop the large stone arches looking out over the city.

"He's probably got the best view of anybody," I said.

We headed down over a little street. "There are lots of churches around here," Nana said. "Up that hill, in behind the trees, is St. Andrew's Presbyterian Church. It's known as The Kirk.

Across the road is Gower Street United Church and down there we have the Anglican Cathedral. That's where we're going. Let's hope we're not late for tea."

Nana took my hand and led me across the busy intersection.

"What do you mean 'for tea'?" I asked.

She smiled. "You'll see."

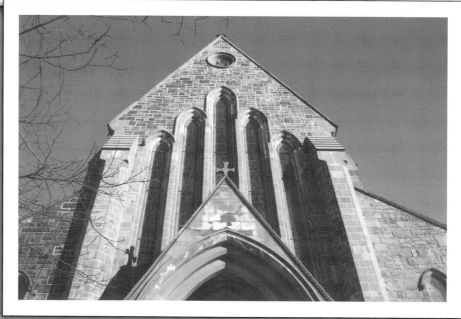

The Cathedral was big and old. I looked up at the narrow, stone towers and stained glass panels. Nana led me through the black, wrought iron gate. It reminded me of a spooky movie, especially when Nana pointed to the cemetery in the churchyard. "It's the oldest one in Canada," she said. "It goes all the way back to 1699." I think she was trying to scare me. But even cemeteries don't look too scary in the daytime.

I was very curious as we headed toward a door on the side of the church instead of the main entrance.

"Are we allowed to go in this way?" I asked.

"Oh, yes. This is the door to the crypt."

"What's a crypt?"

Nana opened her eyes wide and bent down to me. "It's . . . a place . . . where people . . . are buried!" she whispered.

I jumped back but Nana laughed. "Don't worry," she said. "A crypt might have been the original plan, but no one was ever really buried here." She reached for the door and looked back at me. "At least, I don't think so." I held my breath. But then the unexpected happened!

We walked into a beautiful, brightly painted space. Tiny rooms were set with tables covered in lace cloths and adorned with vases of flowers. Nana and I sat at one of the decorated tables. We were served tea with homemade cookies, tarts and buns. I felt very grown up. Once again, Nana had lots of stories. She told me about the Great Fires. I couldn't imagine a city burning down, but it happened to St. John's twice: in 1846 and 1892.

"Back then, Allie, most of the buildings were made of wood, but after the first Great Fire people tried stone and brick thinking it would be safer. Workers carried stone from Signal Hill and even brought it from Ireland to build the Basilica. It took fourteen years to finish the church. It's hard to imagine how they did it considering they didn't have the tools and machinery we have today."

I had lots of questions about the churches and Nana did her best to answer them. I could have sat there for hours, but when we saw the ladies clearing the tables we knew it was time to go.

Monday, August 16th

The weather had been hot and sticky for a week. Nana told me to bring my swimsuit because today we were going to Bowring Park.

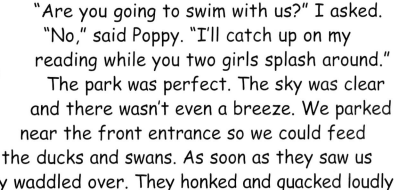

"I'm going to come along, too," Poppy said, picking up the folded blanket and backpack that Nana had put near the front door.

"Are you going to swim with us?" I asked.

"No," said Poppy. "I'll catch up on my reading while you two girls splash around."

The park was perfect. The sky was clear and there wasn't even a breeze. We parked near the front entrance so we could feed the ducks and swans. As soon as they saw us they waddled over. They honked and quacked loudly while I scrambled to untie a bag of birdseed.

"I think they were waiting for us," Poppy said, throwing out a handful of seed.

A swan reached up and pecked the bottom of my T-shirt. "Watch out, Allie," Nana said, laughing. "They can give you quite a nip."

My favourite stop in the Park is the Peter Pan statue. I love finding all the little animals and fairies. "Poppy, how many animals do you think are here?" I asked, circling the statue.

"It's hard to know, because every time I look, I find something new. Which one's your favourite?"

"Hmm. I like the frog . . . but I can't see it now. Oh, and I like this little mouse. It's so cute!"

"Did you see this?" Poppy asked. He read aloud an inscription on the statue: *"Presented to the children of Newfoundland by Sir Edgar R. Bowring in the memory of a dear little girl who loved the park."*

"I've read it before, but what does it mean?" I asked.

"It's to remember a little girl named Betty Munn. She died when the Florizel sank off the coast of Newfoundland in 1918." Poppy stepped back and looked up at Peter Pan. "Did you know that there's another statue like this in Kensington Gardens in London?"

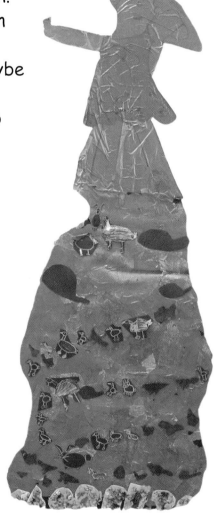

"Really?" I said. "When I go visit Auntie again maybe Uncle Dave will help us find it." I ran my hand over the statue's cool, smooth surface before turning to look for Nana. She waved from the bridge.

"Poppy, where will you be while Nana and I have our swim?"

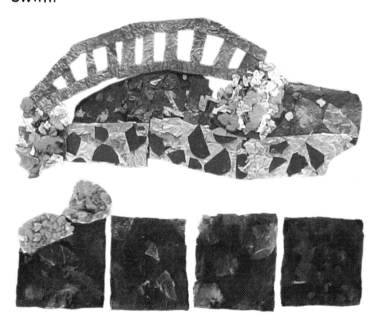

"I'll wait for you girls up here under this lime tree," he said. We walked over to a big beautiful tree. Its leafy branches reached out in all directions. Poppy laid the rolled-up blanket on a nearby bench.

"A lime tree? Do limes really grow on it?" I asked.

Poppy laughed. "No. We don't usually have lime trees in Newfoundland — at least, not like the ones that you find in hot countries. Lime trees are also known as linden trees. This one was specially planted by the Duke of Connaught. Look, it says right here on this plaque: *Lime Tree planted by His Highness the Duke of Connaught on the occasion of the opening of Bowring Park, July 15th, 1914.* How many years ago is that?" he asked, grinning.

"More than 90," Nana answered from behind. "And it's a wonder it's survived the cold of our winters."

We had a wonderful day in Bowring Park. It was hard to leave. Poppy read on the bench while Nana and I had a dip in the pool. I hadn't realized that Nana could even swim, but she was almost as good as me. Next time, we'll definitely have to get Poppy to go.

Tuesday, August 31st

My dad's birthday was coming up. Nana had to buy vegetables because she was planning to cook my dad's favourite meal, Jiggs dinner.

"Let's get the vegetables and salt meat at Lester's Farm," Nana suggested.

"Oh, yes!" I said. "I love that place!"

Lester's Farm is not far from Bowring Park. Mom and Dad always take me there to buy our Halloween pumpkin and to go through the corn maze in the fall. And I love the soft-serve ice-cream.

"The first Farmer Lester," Nana said, "started with a plot of land on the same site about 150 years ago. He had a few cows, horses, pigs and chickens. The Lester family still owns the farm today." Nana took my hand and smiled. "Isn't it wonderful how some things get passed from one generation to another?"

I nodded. "Yes, it's nice when things last a long time."

Lester's was busy as usual. The parking lot was filled. I quickly got out of the car and made my way to the petting barn while Nana and Poppy chatted with Mr. and Mrs. Pike, their neighbours. Everywhere we go Nana *always* stops to talk to someone.

I could hear the little lambs as soon as I ran through the back door of the market. I hurried down the ramp and in through the barn door. A crowd was gathered around a stall. Lying on the straw beneath Buttercup, the goat, was her little baby. He was brand new. His wet coat was a mix of grey and brown. I knew not to go too close, so I just stood back and watched.

"Pretty amazing, isn't it?" the lady next to me said. She had a different accent.

"Yes," I said. "Are you from here?"

"No, we live in New York. We're here on holiday," said the little boy holding her hand.

"New York? Why would you come here for a holiday?"

"We'd heard wonderful things about Newfoundland, and when friends invited us, we couldn't resist," the lady answered. "It's so beautiful! Yesterday we took a boat tour, and tomorrow we're going to Petite Harbour."

"Oh, you mean Petty Harbour. Yeah, it's nice out there," I said. "Have fun. Enjoy your stay."

"Imagine . . . all the way from New York," I muttered as I turned to leave. But, I was beginning to understand why!

I found Nana and Poppy at the counter with a
basket of fresh carrots, turnip, potatoes, cabbage and the salt meat.

Mary, the lady at the counter, twisted the tops off
the carrots. "Would you like to feed the bunnies?"
she asked, handing them over to me with her
usual smile.

"Don't be too long, Allie," Nana called as I
ran past the ice-cream line-up. "Want a
custard cone?"

"Chocolate, please."

Later, Nana and I sat on the front veranda.
"Well, Allie, did you get any ideas for the
quilt?" Nana asked, licking the top off her ice-
cream.

I nodded. "It'll be hard to pick just one."

"Tomorrow we have to stay around the house to prepare your dad's dinner,"
Nana said. "Maybe you can help me cut more fabric pieces and work on the
quilt blocks for Lester's Farm. This is the last stop for our quilt."

"Really?" I said. I couldn't believe it! In just a week my summer vacation
would be coming to an end and I would be heading back to school.

Sunday, September 5th

Today I went with Mom and Dad to see Nana and Poppy. We found them in the kitchen enjoying a cup of tea and reading the paper. "We didn't hear you come in," Nana said. She reached down to give me a hug, and hurried off to her backroom.

  Poppy nodded proudly. "Your grandmother has been burning the midnight oil."

  "Yes, I wanted to have this finished before you went back to school," Nana said, standing in the kitchen doorway. She handed me a huge package.

  I read aloud the attached card:

For a precious granddaughter,
Thank you for your company this summer,
and thanks for helping with another one of
'Nana's Quilts.'

Stitched with Love,
Nana
xoxo

Thursday, September 10th

Back at school, Rebecca had her bag of shells, Anna Marie had her statue of the C.N. Tower, and I had Nana's quilt. I was so proud when my teacher helped me unfold it. I eagerly shared the story of each square: the long hike up Signal Hill, the stroll around Quidi Vidi, the bus ride to Jelly Bean Row, the stories of the churches, the day at Bowring Park and the visit to Lester's Farm.

Wrapped in the comfort of Nana's quilt, I'll always remember Nana and me cutting, ironing and sewing the many pictures of our city, pictures of our summer adventures together.